The Child's Name

Ron Mueller

☙ The Child's Name ❧

By: *Ron Mueller*

Around the World Publishing, LLC
Cincinnati, Ohio 45242

The Child's Name ©

ISBN 13: 978-1-68223-409-9

Distributed by Ingram
Eagle by: © Teekaygee @Dreamstime
Cover Design By: Ron Mueller

Ron Mueller

Dedicated to my Children

The Stories of Taelo are set in the distant past, long before the time currently given as to when people migrated into the western hemisphere.
This is purposely done since the stories are meant to engage the reader in a story and not relate exact history.

The adventures of Taelo and Golden Hawk, sons of White Swan and Quiet Pheasant, provide the backdrop for stories featuring the values of treating others as you wish to be treated, of responsibility, integrity, honesty, contribution, and the joy of learning.

Ron Mueller

The Child's Name

*T*he cool morning air refreshed White Swan as she stepped out of the warmth of her lodge. She along with all the members of the seven sub clans that made up the Elk Clan were camped in this mountain valley by the lake for their annual autumn gathering.

The clans had met here for as long as she could remember but she had listened to the stories of another valley farther to the north where the Elk Clan had first been established. And even more stories about the clan's ancestors coming to a new world across an ice bridge to the north.

She had loved sitting and listening to these stories about these ancestors who had left their land and traveled to a new one. They inspired her and they encouraged her in her pursuit of making a difference for her clan.

White Swan had only fond memories of this long oval valley, surrounded by snow-capped mountains on both sides of a long placid kidney shaped lake where she remembered running and playing as a young girl.

It was where she flirted with the young men in the other sub-clans when she was becoming a young woman. And it was where she had met Grey Fox Running of the Elk Hide Clan. Now she was his mate.

The sun, just breaking over the distant snowcapped mountains, made it appear as if the weeping willows and the cattails on the opposite side of the lake were growing both up into the sky and down into the dark blue lake.

The few grey, pink clouds in the sky were floating above and were also down in the lake.

White Swan admired the panoramic view of the lake framed on its edge by yellowish green willows with a few remaining leaves and a few large round granite boulders all contrasted by the backdrop of the tall lodge pole, darker green pine trees with their thin dark brown flaky bark standing ram rod straight as far as the eye could see.

Suddenly the sound of her totem, a white trumpeter swan broke the morning silence as it crested the hill and flashed white up in the morning sky.

White Swan watched in silence as the brilliant white swan flew down into the valley and the length of the lake and came to a gliding, skimming smooth landing in front of where she stood. It then let out another quieter trumpet and floated over to rest near the large boulder and willow trees on the opposite side of the lake.

Its black beak and bowed white head gave it a grace that White Swan had over the years tried to emulate.

White Swan took the arrival of her totem on the naming day to be something special.

Just then her sister, Quiet Pheasant, joined her.

Together they walked towards the lake to get a closer look at the swan.

They were up early this morning because it was the naming day and they each had a son that would select their names this day.

White Swan realized they had both recovered well from giving birth. She smiled at the thought.

They both had long black hair down to the middle of their backs and were slender and lithe. They were the same height and stood a good head shorter than a spear. Their smooth skin was the color of the autumn grass.

The distinguishing difference between them was the color of their eyes. Quiet Pheasants eyes were walnut brown almost black in color where her own eyes were more golden like a dark honey.

White Swan thought about all the mutual experiences she and Quiet Pheasant shared growing up together in the Elk Horn Clan. They were not only sisters but very close friends. They did almost everything together. This was evident when they met and mated two handsome young ambitious and successful hunters of the Elk Hide Clan.

Their relationships had flourished at the same rate and they had accepted the proposals of these two hunters on the same day.

White Swan thought about the wonderful and sad day when they both moved into the Elk Hide Clan with their mates but left their parents and friends behind.

They had each other and they were quickly accepted into and made friends with their new clan members.

White Swan could not believe the day she went to tell Quite Pheasant the good news and discovered they both had the same news.

They were pregnant!

Then a few months later, on a day very similar this one, the naming day, Quiet Pheasant gave birth to a beautiful baby boy early in the morning and White Swan heard the cry of her son at the peak of the sun's journey across the sky.

The cousin's born on the same day!

White Swan was very conscious of the close relationship the two shared and of the confidence and power they gave each other.

Today was the special day, both of their sons would be placed onto the naming hide to select the object that would determine their name.

****

Far to the north the sun was shining down on the jaggedly scarred face of the Broken Spear the Seer in the Clan of Others. He had a notch missing form his left ear and a scar from the back of his head that met the maze of scars on his face. The sun caused sweat to bead on his forehead and then to slowly run into the corner of his closed eyes.

He had been one of the best hunters in the Clan of the Others. He had been a hunter known as Long Spear until he had defended his hunting team against the attack of a giant brown bear with a notch missing from her left ear.

She had broken his spear, bitten his face, crushed his legs and left him broken and near death.

He had successfully protected his hunting team but had paid a dear price.

His mate nursed him back to life, but it was to be a very changed life.

His new name was Broken Spear. He could no longer hunt but now he talked with the ancestors and often he could see through the eyes of the animals. He had been broken but he had been given a new gift.

At the moment he was now in the mind of an eagle. The Ancestors had summoned him to fly with this eagle so he could see a future leader that would come to the aid of his clan.

In his mind, through the sharp eyes of a white-headed eagle with a spear wide wingspan, the Seer saw the golden wavering sunlight, streaming through the broken clouds, as the morning rays lightly kissed the dark blue placid waters of the oblong lake in the center of a long oval valley surrounded by the foothills of the distant snow peaked mountains.

The Broken Spear estimated the lake to be a hefty spear's throw wide and at least twenty spear throws long. Cattail plants with their stems turned a pale tan with dried leaves and topped with reddish brown sausage like seed pods bordered its banks.

A mix of willows of all sizes completed the border of the lake. He could make out several large grey granite boulders that could serve as sitting or diving spots.

A lone white swan floated near a stand of yellowing cattails.

The eagle was riding the up draft as the air warmed by the early morning sun rose from the valley rim. The eagle was determined to only focus on one thing, whereas the Seer wanted to see all. He tried to control where the eagle looked but the eagle fought to keep its eyes on its one target.

The will of the eagle was very strong. The seer knew something special was about to happen, but he did not know what it would be.

****

The naming ceremony had started. White Swan, with her young child sitting in the seat formed by her crossed legs, sat quietly, and leaned against Grey Fox Running. Next to her was Quiet Pheasant, sitting in the same way with her child and leaning against Red Oak.

Her cheek on Grey Fox Running's shoulder, White Swan felt a warmth pass into her that was the feeling of contentment and peace.

She knew that her sister shared the same close bond with her mate.

White Swan wished her sister the same warm feeling that she had now.

White Swan was pleased that the children of all the births that had taken place thirty moon cycles ago had survived and were present for the naming ceremony.

The length of time before a name was given to a child had been decided long ago by the council of elders. It was believed that a child with a name carried the burdens of this world into land of the ancestors.

A child without a name carried no burdens and would be raised by the ancestors.

In past cycles, many children went to the ancestors with no burdens but not this time.

White Swan looked at the naming hide and the objects around its edges. Each child would be placed on the naming hide and each would select an object. This object and the child's past behaviors and actions would guide the elders and parents in selecting a final name.

White Swan looked around at the twelve children who would be selecting their object from the edge of the naming hide. The child with the most moon and sun cycles was first.

White Swan relaxed and prepared to watch each of the children.

Her son was number twelve. She would be last to hand her son to the elder sitting in the center of the naming hide.

White Swan felt the presence and heard the quite talking and watched the movement of the members of the seven sub-clans that made up the Elk clan.

They were sitting attentively all around the outside of the circle of the proud parents of the twelve to be named. The clan participation and encouragement of the young ones making the selection was part of the ceremony.

The volume and participation of the clan members was triggered by an indecisive child. This would give fuel to friends to shout out what the child should select.

The gathering seemed to relish the indecisive child.

All morning the eagle circled the valley.

The sun was almost at its zenith when White Swan looked up and seemed to look directly into the piercing yellow eyes that seemed focused on her. She imagined feeling the edge of the sharp orange beak capable of effortlessly ripping through the hide of an elk.

The eagle's white head feathers ended at the leading edge of its wings and the feathers at the ends of its spear length black wings were spread like the fingers of an open hand and were wavering as the air currents passed by them.

Its yellow claws were closed and tucked below the broad white tail that deftly guided its easy floating glide. She made note of the eagles very large size and absorbed its flowing splendor, acknowledged its dominance of the air, and then turned her attention back to the ceremony.

She had been distracted but quickly refocused when she realized that Quiet Pheasant and Red Oak were standing up to hand their young one to the elder.

He who would show the child each object spaced around the reddish-brown fox fur that was the trim around a two-spear diameter circular tan brushed elk hide.

For the eleventh time White Swan examined all the rocks of various colors, leaves, pieces of wood, bones, scraps of hide from numerous animals, feathers and feet of birds that would be waved back and forth three times in front of the child and then placed on the fox fur trim of the naming hide.

Some articles were colorfully decorated. Some were plain. Each had a meaning and would influence the name given to the child.

White Swan noted that most of the young chose the colorful objects. Long ago on this same naming hide she had chosen the white feather of the trumpeter swan.

Quiet Pheasant had chosen the feather of a pheasant. Quiet Pheasant, like Grey Fox Running had earned a second part to their names because of the observations made by their parents or the elders.

White Swan smiled as she thought about the many times her mother had threatened to add a second name for her and call her Stubborn Swan. She was the person her mother knew to be determined and stubborn but known to all only as White Swan.

White Swan released an involuntary whispering *"yes"* of approval as Quiet Pheasant's young one picked the feather of the golden hawk.

It was a symbol of bravery and leadership.

Black hair, tall and slender for his age and eyes like his mother the young boy held his feather high as he walked back toward his parents. He would have a distinctive name. Good choice, young *Golden Hawk*, White Swan thought as she stood up to give him and Quiet Pheasant a hug.

Quiet Pheasant's beaming face warmed White Swan's heart.

White Swan stood and her young one toddled over to his best friend and touched the feather.

White Swan noted that the two boys looked much the same. Her son was just a little taller with eyes very much like hers but with a distinct almost black edge around dark honey brown eyes. Both boys would be as tall as their fathers.

Grey Fox Running was congratulating his best friend Red Oak as White Swan gave her sister a hug.

It was her son's turn.

White Swan took note that he had been born and was now picking his name when the sun was at its zenith.

He was last and it was clear the elder was tired and he seemed relieved that the naming ceremony was coming to the end. He took the last child and began to show him all the objects before placing him in the center of the naming circle.

White Swan and Grey Fox Running watched as their son was slowly turned and shown all the articles. The elder then placed him in the center of the hide and stepped out of the circle.

The loud noise arising from the lake caused all to turn and look to where White Swan's totem was flapping its wings on the water and repeatedly trumpeting.

The eagle's piercing gaze turned to seek its goal and found what it had been patiently waiting for. Letting out an ear-splitting scream, the eagle folded his wings and shot like an a spear down, down ever so swiftly down, toward its target.

****

At the same moment but far to the North the sweat caused Broken Spear's eyes to burn, and his pulsing scars were now dark red or purple and as hard as he tried to see the boy, all he could see through the eyes of the eagle was the claw of an eagle.

He did not understand. He was confused and frustrated.

He needed to see the boy, but the eagle's eyes were glued to its prize.

****

Instinct caused White Swan to turn her gaze from the lake back to where her son was standing. She froze in terrified fear as she watched the eagle's spear like descent toward her son who was standing in the center of the naming hide with an eagle's claw held high to the sky.

The boy and eagle clearly saw each other and nothing else.

The clan members were once again distracted as the white swan on the lake began a running wing flapping dance as it ran across the surface of the water and finally rose smoothly into the air and began a slow graceful flight around the valley.

White Swan did not look out to the lake but instinctively moved to save her son as the eagle swooped swiftly down and miraculously plucked the claw from the small up stretched hand.

Firmly clasping its prize in its claws and letting out another much closer ear-piercing cry, it opened its wings and rose swiftly upwards toward the clouds in the sky.

The boy had chosen the eagle's claw and the eagle had accepted it and by its action had chosen the boy.

The clan members turned their eyes back from the lake in time to see the exchange and then watched as the eagle rose into the sky with its prize. The white swan of equal wingspan and size gracefully followed as the eagle flew out of the valley.

For the first time during the ceremony there was silence. Nothing like this had ever happened before.

****

Far away the Seer shook his head as the vision from the mind of the eagle ended. He had tried to see the boy. The eagle had focused only on the claw. The ancestors had foretold that this young one chosen by the eagle would someday save his clan. But where was this young boy and who was he and when would the clan need saving? The Seer knew he would have to wait for the next vision, message from the ancestors or for time to pass.

****

Tears of joy ran down White Swan's cheeks into the lightly pine scented hair of her son as she hugged him to her bosom. She had feared the eagle would either take her son or hurt him.

The opening of the eagle's wings had totally hidden her son and for a moment total fear had overtaken her. Then she watched the eagle take the claw from the small hand. The eagles cry seemed to say thank you.

The strong arms of Grey Fox Running encircled them both and completed the union of the three as they knelt in the middle of the naming hide.

Golden Hawk squeezed in to give his best friend a hug and Quiet Pheasant and Red Oak all joined in, as together the two couples knelt in the center of the naming hide.

White Swan, tears of joy streaming down her cheek, thought about the choice of the claw of the eagle. She knew it represented leadership, power, skill, and bravery.

She wondered what else it foretold.

Normally there was a waiting period until the child's name was picked but in this case the eagle had determined the name. Her son was the claw of the eagle or *Taelo* in the language of the clan.

She stood up, held her son up and proudly introduced him as *Taelo* (Tā low) to all the clan members and Quiet Pheasant stood, held her son up and introduced *Golden Hawk*.

This was a first for the clan and it foretold of many firsts that Taelo and Golden Hawk would deliver to the clan.

And so, thousands of years ago the adventures of Taelo and Golden Hawk began.

Thank you for reading this story.

About the Author

Ronald E. Mueller
remwriter95@gmail.com

Ron grew up in what is now Flint River State Park in Southeast Iowa. The 170-year-old house Ron lived in is built into a hillside. It faces a 125-foot-high cliff towering over the little Flint River. The house and the land talked to him about; the passing of time, the struggle to conquer the land, the struggles people faced and the wonder of nature.

He climbed the cliffs, crawled into the caves, dove from the swimming rock, collected clams from the bottom of the pond, gigged and skinned frogs for their legs. He trapped muskrats for fur, hunted raccoon in the dead of night, and with only a stick hunted rabbits in the dead of winter.

His young life was outdoors, and nature tested him.

He walked to a one room stone schoolhouse uphill both ways. A stern but warm-hearted teacher, Mrs. Henry was instrumental in shaping his character as she shepherded him from the fourth to the eighth grade.

It was a great way to grow up.

Ron graduated from Burlington, High School, went to Vietnam in the Navy. He graduated from The University of South Florida with a master's degree in engineering, worked for thirty eight years for Procter and Gamble, traveled around the world thirty times.

He has remained happily married for more than fifty years. His daughter and his two sons are all successful and his three grandchildren have all graduated.

His wife has humored and supported him as he became a full time professional story teller.

His experiences inter-twined with snippets of fantasy lend themselves to the adventures he leads the reader through.

Ron Mueller

Books by Ron Mueller
Fiction Series
The Taelo Series
The Early Years
The Golden Feather
Journey of Discovery
Dangerous Passage
Condor Clan Slingers
Circumvention
The Journey of Sages
Future Leaders Journey
Taelo Collection

A Taelo Story
White Swan and Quiet Pheasant
The Child's Name
Floating Cloud
Quiet Rabbit
Busy Bee
Little Otter & Talking Wren
Broken Spear
Burley Bear & Meadow Flower
Taelo Story Collection

The Alex Evercrest Series
The River Front
The Girl on The Grill
Missing
Maggot
Racist
Votive Candles
Windy City
Country Road
Pool of Blood
Sins of the Daughter
Body Parts
The Skull Collector
The Vanishing
The Shadow Fighter
Moonshine
Grief's Trajectory
The Magic Touch
Northern Lights
Alex Evercrest Heroine
Alex Evercrest Collection Two
New Direction
A Family Affair
Disruption
The St. Lebuinnus Church Murder

A Brian O'Neil Novel
Hawaiian Phoenix
Moon Curser
Death Broker

The Problem Solver Series
Solutions
Drug Lords
Border Crosser
The Problem Solver Collection

16

Science Fiction
The Savitar Series:
Journey's End
Savitar
Confluence
Savitar Series Collection

Bram Nielson Series
The Fold
The Message
Fold Wormhole
Negative Fold
Ripples in Time
Bram Nielson Collection

Single Science Fiction Books:
Current Past and Future
The Event
The Door
Viajante 7

https://www.remwriter95.net/

Ron Mueller

Around the world Publishing, LLC